Message to Parents

Bear & Company, part of The Boyds Collection, Ltd. family, is committed to creating quality reading and play experiences that inspire kids to learn, imagine, and explore the world around them. Working together with experienced children's authors, illustrators, and educators, we promise to create stories and products that are respectful to your children that will earn your respect in turn.

Welcome to
the World of
Digby in Disguise™!

The world can be scary when you're just a little bear. But with a little magic and make-believe, even the littlest bear can do amazing things!

To Greg, Jonathan, Adam, and Noah

~ KD Wurtz

For Allison, Gretchen, and Pammy, whose friendship
means the world to me

~ Tracey D. Carrier

Published by Bear & Company Publications
Copyright © 2002 by Bear & Company

        Permissions
        Bear & Company Publications
        P.O. Box 3876
        Gettysburg, PA 17325

Printed in the United States of America

Digby In Disguise™ and Digby Little Bear™ are registered trademarks of Bear & Company.

Based on a series concept by Dawn Jones
Edited by Dawn Jones
Designed by Vernon Thornblad

Library of Congress Cataloging-in-Publication Data
Wurtz, K. D. (Katherine Danielle), 1964-
  Digby finds a friend / by K.D. Wurtz ; illustrated by Tracey D.
Carrier.
        p. cm. -- (Digby in disguise ; 2)
Summary: When Digby wants to make a new friend he turns to his
disguises, but he does not need them in the end.
  ISBN 0-9712840-2-4
  [1. Bears--Fiction. 2. Friendship--Fiction. 3. Neighbors--Fiction.] I.
Carrier, Tracey Dahle, ill. II. Title. III. Series.
  PZ7.W9658 Dg 2002
  [E]--dc21
                        2001005071

Digby
Finds a Friend

By KD Wurtz   Illustrated by Tracey D. Carrier

bear&
company™

Digby the little bear looked out the window at the house where his friend Jonah used to live. He did not even notice the butterflies that fluttered among the daisies.

Ever since Jonah moved away Digby had been wishing for a new friend.

Now his wish was coming true.

A little girl bear and her family were going to live next door.

Just then, a tiny car loaded with boxes of every size and shape came around the corner.

"They're here!" Digby cried.

Digby followed Momma outside. She walked next door to say hello. But Digby stood on the front porch and stared over the railing.

The car door opened, and someone stepped out.

Suddenly, it was as if the butterflies in the garden had moved into Digby's furry tummy.

This new little bear was no ordinary bear. She had wings that shimmered in the sun, a pretty crown of flowers, and sparkling brown eyes. She looked like she had come from fairyland.

Digby hugged his teddy bear to his chest. "It will be a bazillion, gazillion years before she wants me to be her friend," he whispered to Teddy.

"Digby," Momma called from next door, "come and meet Molly."

But Digby didn't answer. Molly was beautiful and magical, and he wasn't magical at all.

He was just a little bear.

Digby decided that before he met Molly, there was something he had to do. He ran inside to his room and opened the big, blue trunk that sat in the corner.

Nana had given Digby this wonderful trunk to help him when he was bored or lonely, happy or sad, angry or scared.

Digby thrust both furry paws into the trunk. It had worked before. So now he was sure he'd find just the right thing to help him with Molly.

He did.

In the flutter of a butterfly's wing, Digby, the little bear who wasn't magical enough to be friends with a fairy, was gone.

In his place stood

Digby the Great,

a wondrous wizard.

The wizard turned and ran from the house to meet his magical new friend. "I am the wondrous wizard, Digby the Great," he said grandly when he reached Molly.

Digby took Molly by the paw. Before she could say a word, he pulled her up the steps to her new home. He had something to show her.

Digby the Great tapped the front door three times with his wand. He said the magic words

"Shala, Shala, Inka, Boom!"

Then he opened the door.

Inside, there were flowers and balloons everywhere—and a sign that read

"Welcome."

Molly looked amazed. Digby the Great smiled.

"I can do more magic," he told the little fairy quickly. Molly didn't answer. She just walked into the house and started looking around.

"I'll go get my assistant, Teddy," said Digby. He knew she'd be even more amazed when he made Teddy vanish—

POOF!

Digby couldn't wait to show her.

But when Digby the Great got back to Molly's house with his assistant, Molly was sitting on her mother's lap.

She looked sad.

"Don't worry," Molly's mother was saying. "We'll just have to find some wonderful new things for your room. Then this house will start to feel just as special as our old house."

Digby the Great turned around and walked slowly back home to his room. The wand and hat disappeared inside his trunk.

Molly didn't need more magic.

Digby the little bear sat down on his bed to think. What Molly needed was

something special—
something extra-special—

something that would make the house next-door so wonderful that she would never want to leave.

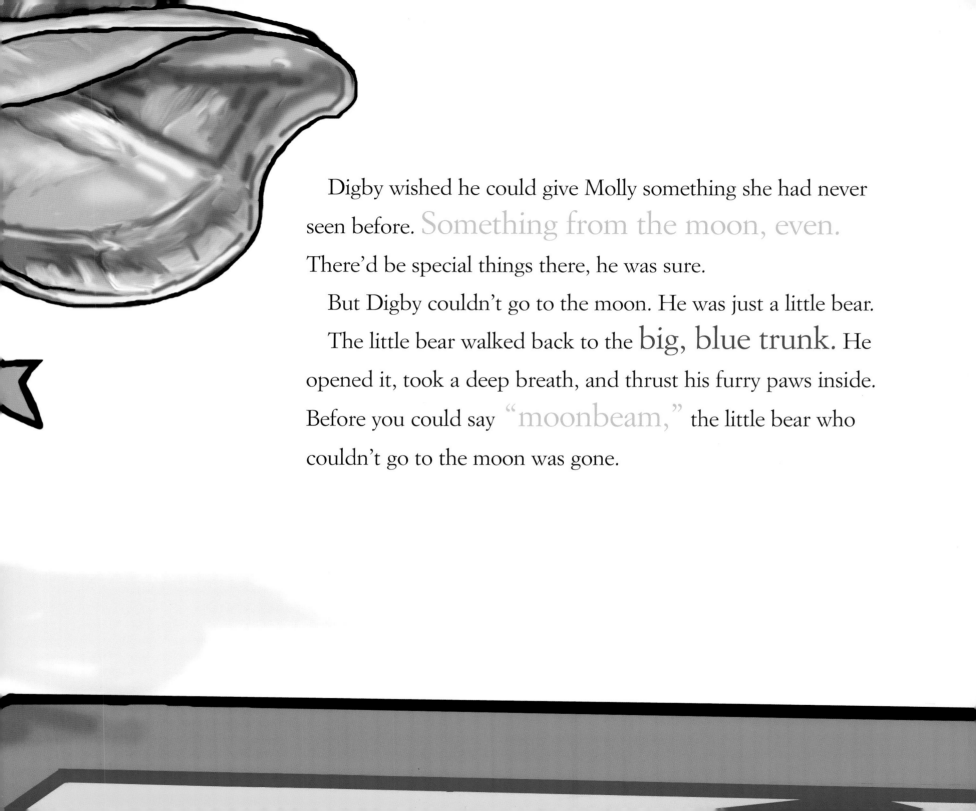

Digby wished he could give Molly something she had never seen before. Something from the moon, even. There'd be special things there, he was sure.

But Digby couldn't go to the moon. He was just a little bear.

The little bear walked back to the big, blue trunk. He opened it, took a deep breath, and thrust his furry paws inside. Before you could say "moonbeam," the little bear who couldn't go to the moon was gone.

In his place stood

Astronaut Digby.

Astronaut Digby climbed bravely into his rocket and
took off for the moon.

He could tell right away that the moon was a wonderful place
with lots of special things! He saw a silver moon
butterfly flitting through the air. He saw pale-
purple moonflowers climbing over the
gray rocks.

Astronaut Digby looked everywhere for just the
right thing to take back to Molly. Then he saw
it—a perfectly round stone the color
of moonlight. He smiled and flew from his
rocket to grab it.

When Digby looked up, he saw another astronaut coming around a moon boulder.

It was Molly.

She knew how to get to the moon, too!

Digby started to smile. But then he thought of something. That meant she probably had a million moon-stones already. His wasn't special at all. He let the moonstone drop from his paw.

"There you are!"

Digby looked up into Astronaut Molly's happy brown eyes. "Do you want to play with me?" she asked.

"I don't know," said Digby. "I'm not magical like you. I'm just a little bear. And you've already been to the moon. I don't know where else to go to find something special to give you. So now you don't have anything special for your new house."

"Yes, I do," Molly said as she took off her helmet. "I have a friend. You filled my new house with those beautiful flowers. And you came all the way to the moon for me."

"I did, didn't I?" said the little bear with a smile.

Molly nodded. Then she put her astronaut suit next to Digby's. She reached down for her new friend's paw and pulled him to his feet.

Together, the two ordinary but happy little bears ran off to play in the blue spring air.